Yet There *Is Room*

A Story of Redemption

Marion Roybal

ISBN 978-1-64458-959-5 (paperback)
ISBN 978-1-64458-960-1 (digital)

Copyright © 2019 by Marion Roybal

All rights reserved. No part of this publication may be reproduced, distributed, or transmitted in any form or by any means, including photocopying, recording, or other electronic or mechanical methods without the prior written permission of the publisher. For permission requests, solicit the publisher via the address below.

Christian Faith Publishing, Inc.
832 Park Avenue
Meadville, PA 16335
www.christianfaithpublishing.com

Printed in the United States of America

In loving memory of Lawrence Ray Troupe

Preface

King Solomon wrote: "Of the making of many books there is no end" (Eccl. 12:12b). There are indeed many books, more than Solomon could have ever imagined; but there are far more stories that have never found their way into books. Whether these are true or imaginary, many of us wish to communicate something to present or future generations. The idea for the following story began in the imagination of a man with a wonderfully creative and gifted mind; but disease plagued him for most of his adult life, finally culminating in a stroke that robbed him of sight and will. I am writing this story in his memory.

When *Roe v. Wade* was passed in 1973, he imagined a story about an encounter between an abortionist, Dr. Paul Boresman, who was killed in a car crash, and a now-young girl Carlee, one of the many unborn who had died at his hands. The conversation takes place somewhere between earth and heaven, in a great and blindingly bright gulf. After being aborted, Carlee had been taken into custody by her Heavenly Father and grew and matured under his nurturing and loving care. God allows her to spend time with Paul Borseman to satisfy her curiosity about the process of human thought and decision, particularly how man, God's crowning creation, brings itself to conclusions so contrary to those of the Creator. For the child, the interchange is about discovery; for the doctor, it is about the damnable debate, choice versus prolife.

Solomon also wrote: "For God will bring every deed into judgment, including every hidden thing, whether good or bad" (Eccl. 12:14). The cancerous blemish on the human heart is the willingness to kill, not the criminals who rob us of life and liberty but rather the most vulnerable, fragile, innocent, and dependent members of our society: the unborn. These we eliminate for the sake of convenience or, in some cases, of fear and ignorance and, worse yet, of malice. The following story is obviously fiction and not intended to impart any new revelation about the afterlife itself or about what happens to aborted babies. We know, however, that God, who does all things well, is doing what is just and right for these defenseless little ones, the ones for whom we are supposed to speak. By virtue of who he is, God cannot and will not turn a blind eye to the secret and blatant evil deeds of men or turn a deaf ear to the silent cry of the unborn, whose lives are taken in their mothers' wombs.

We humans struggle with concepts of justice and injustice, wishing we had the liberty to mete out punishment of our own choosing for crimes and criminals. However, "Vengeance is mine," says the Lord. When the Lord was approaching the time of his death, he sent his disciples into a Samaritan village to make preparations for the Passover meal, but the people of Samaria did not welcome them because they were going to Jerusalem. James and John were so indignant that they asked the Lord if they should call down fire from heaven to destroy them (just as Elijah had in the Old Testament). Jesus's response was merely to rebuke them (Lk. 9:55f). Oh, to have been a fly on the wall during that conversation. We are not told exactly what the rebuke was, but two things seem evident: the disciples were presumptive in even thinking they had that kind of power, and secondly, "Vengeance is mine," says the Lord. In his time, God will judge, and he alone has the power and the authority to do so. But judgment is God's "strange" work: "The Lord will rise up as he did at Mount Perazim, he will rouse himself as in the Valley of Gibeon to do his work, his strange work, and perform his task, his alien task" (Isa. 28:21). The work he loves to do is to save; and so he does, freely and richly. God's ways are unsearchable and just, far above our ways; and we are called to trust him. Justice is his to dispense as is his salvation.

Over a hundred years ago, a minister of the Word of God named Joseph Parker, DD, wrote a commentary on Leviticus and Numbers. As he expounds on God's command to Moses to count the people of Israel, he writes these words:

How was the numbering to proceed? Every man was of consequence. We think we honour God by speaking of him *only* [emphasis mine] as the Lord of Creation, the God of Hosts, the Ruler of incalculable armies stretching over spaces infinite; it is our poverty of thought that so strains itself as to lay hold of what to us are great numbers; God rather seeks to glorify himself in counting men one by one. "The very hairs of your head are all numbered." Looking round his banqueting table, he says, "Yet, there is room." He seems to notice the vacancies as certainly and as clearly as he notices the occupants. To us, numbers are alone of consequence; to our Father, the one child is of great importance: saith he, "One is wanting; go fetch him; call more loudly for him; the next appeal may strike his ear and elicit the response of his heart; go out again, and again, and rather blame the darkness of the night than the unwillingness of the child; give him one more opportunity.

This story is about the one given an opportunity to come to the table and eat with the Savior even as he faces death and a girl named Carlee.

Chapter 1

The melding of steering wheel, dashboard, and glass with his body culminated in an instant of grinding finality. There was the fleeting fascination with the *impossibility* of such a sudden stop and the simultaneous *possibility* that death had come to claim him. And there was the matter of the truck that appeared out of nowhere, crowding his little car off the road. Considering the many unanswered questions and nagging doubts that surrounded Dr. Paul Boresman's forty-seven years, the knowledge of death's absolute surety was about to crystallize within the space between here and gone.

But gone to where?

The expensive, fragile, speeding car failed to penetrate the concrete retaining wall or fall away as one might suppose would happen. Instead, it lingered tight against the wall, an ugly, mangled distortion of its original design. That he couldn't remember the name of the car was unimportant; the notion that death alone survived dominated his thoughts, and so he waited. Waited for what, he did not know.

As if in a dream, thoughts of his wife and a dinner party drifted across his consciousness and then passed. Dr. Paul Boresman, dead and on hold—his personal significance and all that had mattered just thirty seconds ago quickly losing all importance, all taking flight like dry, dead leaves raked by an October wind. His whole life drifted slowly before him as if he were watching a slideshow. He saw his childhood, his parents smiling at him so proudly as he graduated from grade school, high school, and medical school. Snippets of memories flew out at him, some that saddened and embarrassed him, others that brought joy and happiness. He was standing with Jennifer at the altar as they vowed to love and cherish each other until death parted them. He wanted to dwell on that for a moment. He didn't intend for it to be this way. But the show went on. Michael and Julie, babies and then walking and running and graduating from high school. He saw a physician, a handsome man in a white jacket, smiling as a parade of women walked past him—his patients. And then the show was over. Is this what is meant when they, whoever *they* are, say that at the moment of death, your whole life flashes before your eyes, the condensed version? Or was life really that short? It seemed so now. And what about now? He wondered why he felt no sense of anticipation about what was ahead. He always had heard that this entrance into the next life stimulated expectation, wonderment, adventure, reward; but there was none of that, none of that now, only a sense of uncertainty, solitude, and fear. The nature of that fear could never have been expected; it was filling him, crowding out every thought. There seemed to be no room for anything but fear itself. He struggled for one piece of reality that could drag him back, but it wouldn't come. *What was the name of my car?*

His senses of substance and stability were becoming fluid; he indeed had become unsubstantial. Oddly, he had presence of mind and that, barely, but nothing else. Briefly, he wondered why he felt no pain. He was being carried along on a journey of sorts, and he had neither the will nor the means to direct the route. He had a sense of being upright on nothing he could see or feel. An aura of light surrounded him, but he could see no source; he felt no air movement, and he heard no sounds. He willed to lift his arms to look at his hands, to feel around him; but to his horror, there were none. He wasn't even a shadow; he was nothing except a collection of thoughts and an acute sense of awareness. *I know*, he thought, *I'm dreaming. This is a bad dream, and when I awaken, I will be in my own bed, in my own home.* Then he remembered the accident, and the shocking reality of death returned to him. How could this be? He wasn't ready. If he was in hell—and he certainly had done nothing to deserve hell—even the thought made him feel indignant. Where was the fire, the screaming, that horned creature, the devil, with a long sweeping tail? He immediately dismissed that idea, but he saw nothing that looked like heaven either—no angels, no music, no God. He concluded that all the ideas he had ever heard about heaven and hell were wrong, merely the product of someone's sadistic imagination or wishful thinking. *This is it? Nothing—a vast expanse of nothingness, save a nearly blinding brightness and a deafening silence?* This, he was sure, was worse than any hell could ever be! The fear he had felt a moment ago paled in comparison to what he began to feel. Not only had it filled him, but it was also spilling out of him. Terror, desperation, and loneliness were piercing his mind like electric shocks, and he was helpless, at the mercy of—

Chapter 2

Suddenly, he sensed a presence outside of himself. At first, it appeared to be just a mist forming in the light nothingness, but then it began to take shape as it neared him. With tremendous relief sweeping over his overwrought mind, he saw that it was a person, small, willowy, more feminine than masculine, but, nonetheless, a person. It seemed weightless as it gracefully and purposefully moved toward him. The light parted like fragile transparent curtains wafting in a gentle breeze, making way for the being. Perhaps he had overreacted. Perhaps this interlude of frightening emptiness was just temporary, and now he would be rescued. But again he was confused about seeing and yet without eyes. Nothing was making sense to him. *What if this is just a figment of my imagination, a wraith appearing to a confused and desperate, dying mind?* Again he considered raising a hand to touch his eyes or to reach out to the nearing figure, but then he remembered that he had no hands with which to touch anything—an unprecedented nightmare. Everything was surreal, and he had no choice but to be swept along with it. The scene surpassed any science fiction he had ever read, and it certainly overruled any form of science he had ever studied. "Someone has to answer for this. I am a physician, an educated man!" he shouted like a frustrated child, his voice penetrating the silence and echoing back at him. *How could that be?* he wondered briefly. Before he could consider the enigma further, he focused all his attention on the creature that continued to drift toward him. It was saying something. At least its mouth was moving. No doubt, the mellow and reassuring voice was directed at him and was distinctly feminine or boyish; he couldn't tell, and it was truly inconsequential in this moment.

"Hello, Paul Boresman. My name is Carlee, and I can only imagine what you are feeling right now, and certainly your frustration is understandable considering the trauma you have just experienced." She was definitely talking to him and doing so with a level of assurance one might have who is interviewing a potential employee. For the time being, he would let it pass that she had neglected to call him *Dr.* Paul Boresman. "Please, bear with me. Trust me, and soon enough, all that you are experiencing will become clear. It is more or less useless for you to resist and struggle against what, as you have concluded, is not in your control," she continued as if it made no difference whether or not he was in agreement with her. To say it in the meanest of terms, she definitely had the upper hand. Though he certainly did not agree with the direction that his life had taken a few minutes ago, he seemed to lack any will whatsoever to interrupt her or change the course of these moments. And to have something outside of himself, or what was left of himself, was a tremendous relief for the moment. She calmly announced, "You are indeed dead, and coming to grips with that reality will make our conversation more fruitful. I am asking you to believe me. I am very real, and I am here with you because I have been given permission." She was going on, talking nonsense as far as he was concerned. *Hard facts, fruitful, permission. Permission from whom and for what purpose, and what about moving on from here? Certainly, I must have to be somewhere,* he thought as she continued on in her controlled, lilting voice.

And then as if she was reading his mind, she said, "I should add that time is no longer a consideration. We are not on the clock, so to speak." A faint smile crossed her lips, but it quickly faded. Her words flowed easily as if she had rehearsed them many times. She was unearthly and yet earthly and way too confident for his taste.

He wanted to laugh, to let go with a long loud, hysterical, mirthless laugh, such as one might do who just found out that his business partner had been stealing him blind, leaving him dead broke, but is very sorry and wants to know if they can go out for dinner and talk about old times. *Laugh or cry—crying will make me too vulnerable. I hate feeling vulnerable.*

Paul Boresman, medical doctor of women's health, certified OB-GYN. He had everything a man could ever want: a beautiful wife, a three-story home on five acres, two good kids, and a sports car, a red Miata, a status symbol that put him in the "cut above" crowd. And here he was, for the first time in his life, not in control.

And what did she say her name was? Carlee? And why am I stuck here with someone I don't even know and yet seems to know me? I'm positive that I don't know her. Carlee. No. No one by that name has crossed my path. I'd remember that name, an unusual name. "I'm afraid you've lost me, uh, Carlee. I'm not following you, and I wonder if I could, uh, ask you a few questions first just to clarify, perhaps?" he stumbled. Again his own voice surprised him, a voice and no body from which it could come.

Carlee continued on as if he hadn't spoken, "You spent a whole lifetime denying the obvious, and that makes the obvious difficult to recognize. You have always been in control, haven't you?" The question did not require an answer. "Dr. Boresman, in your profession, you were surrounded by the obvious. All that you studied and learned and experienced pointed to an orderly, creative mind, but you resisted. Do you remember the moment when you considered the notion of truth, but you pressed it back and down until it slipped away from you, never to surface again?"

He did not answer her, but instead he became very focused on the accident. He couldn't go into any kind of philosophical dialogue until he had a clear picture in his mind of what had happened to him.

Again, she seemed to know what he was thinking and said, "Come and see." She appeared to be looking down at something, and suddenly he was looking with her.

"Is that my car, my Miata?" Yes, there it was, the name of his precious car! He was relieved to remember but horrified to see no semblance of his sporty red toy, just a mass of misshapen metal and glass and blood—a lot of blood. Emergency vehicles, as well as police and medical personnel, surrounded the scene. He felt close enough to reach out and touch the red metal, if he had hands, and yet it was so far away. All wrong—this was all wrong.

The girl spoke, breaking his thoughts to pieces, "Yes, that was your car. Your body is still in there. Watch as they frantically try to pull you free. They hope you are alive, but we know differently, don't we?" She spoke with incredible kindness as if she was grieving for him, as if she really cared for him.

The questions, always asking me questions. I should be doing the asking here, not she. I am the victim. He spit out a reply, "Because we are watching this, do you expect me to agree to be dead?" As silly as the words sounded to him, he meant it.

With complete control and not even a hint of defensiveness, she replied, "It doesn't matter whether you agree or not. The business of agreeing is only pertinent if both parties have a grasp of the same reality. For instance, traffic is no problem here, not a reality as you knew it to be just moments ago." She moved her arms outward away from her small body as if she was pointing to something that he wasn't able to see. "In fact, the only reality here is truth. Nothing else exists outside of relationship with him who is truth."

"Are you trying to tell me that the reason that I am here, that I was 'killed' so violently, is to get to the truth? Are all my questions about life about to be answered?" A hint of sarcasm flavored his query. "Then I will be able to move ahead and get to the business of reward or whatever it is that I am to get." It was no question. He still clung to some thread of hope that he was in control.

"No, not at all. I mean you were not 'killed' so that you could be here, but rather, you are here because you were in a car crash," she said. "You are only passing through. Where you will go from here is not up to me, and I am not going on your journey."

He sensed that she knew something he didn't, and a rush of anger surged through him. "My journey? Who says I want to embark on a journey? If I will to, can't I opt out?" He didn't wait for an answer. How was he to refuse anything? He felt somewhat foolish in view of the fact that he had no legs with which to run, and the landscape was light and nothingness as far as his mind's eye could see. Indeed, he felt very foolish and helpless as a newborn babe.

Chapter 3

He was slowly but surely coming to grips with the fact that his choices had all been made. As if he thought he might gain a mite of an edge, he began to engage the girl creature in a philosophical discussion, an arena in which he was quite comfortable. He would distract her, perhaps impress on her just how intelligent and wise he was, all the while finding out her motive for detaining him. "Are you saying that I am about to make that great leap into full knowledge? Don't I remember someone saying we are all special, unique, that we all climb to greater and greater heights, but our uniqueness takes us on different pathways? Well, I think I can really get into this—the adventure, the discovery, and all. Are you my guide?"

"Not exactly," she responded with a slight hesitation in her voice. There was that smile. He didn't care much for that knowing smile she gave him. She continued, "I think in your lifetime, there was an exaggeration of your 'specialness.' Instead of recognizing something greater than yourself, you stopped short. As I said before, there was that moment of truth that you discarded just before discovery could free you. You labored through your short life content to be confined to a world that you created with you and only what mattered to you: in the center."

"Well, even so," he defended, "the world is full of people such as myself. We are what make the world a good place in which to live. I didn't gain success and a life of privilege by allowing myself to be one at the bottom of the pile. I was taught to push upward and that if I didn't do it, no one would do it for me." He was surprised at the edge of pride in his voice. He pressed back a sense of embarrassment that had crept up on him; and though he felt restless and insecure in the presence of this girl, he intended to finish with some self-respect. He couldn't let her see him as weak or easily broken. He was even more disgusted with himself for having had an apologetic thought about his life and the way in which he lived it. "Could we get on with this, whatever it is we are supposed to accomplish?" he snapped.

The girl moved closer to him and with eyes as clear as a summer sky gazed into what he could only assume were the eyes of his soul and responded, "There is something you need to understand." Her tone was terribly sad, and that did not comfort him. "You are not here to accomplish anything, at least not with me. The reason you are here is not for your benefit but rather for mine."

His mind leaped at the thought of gaining ground, so to speak, and he quickly responded, "Ah, well, how can I help?" *Now we are getting somewhere. This poor girl needs some answers,* he mused, feeling a little more hopeful about the moment.

"As a doctor, you were always ready to help others, at least in the beginning."

"What do you mean in the beginning?" he interrupted. "My whole practice was about helping people. Surely, that has not gone unnoticed here!" His dignity was wounded.

She smiled softly, caringly, lifting her hand as if to reach for him. He was suddenly envious of her substance, her solidity. He longed to touch or feel something. "Now, Dr. Boresman, we are getting close to the reason you are here. Did you take pride in your ability to recognize your patients, you know, remember their individual ailments, their names, important information about them that made them feel special and significant?"

"Oh yes! We kept excellent records, of course, and yes, on the whole, we trained ourselves to remember our patients. Of course, you need to recognize that I saw hundreds of patients and some of them only once. Certainly, you aren't intimating that I could remember everyone, are you? But I reiterate: I have an excellent memory."

"Then surely you remember me," she said firmly. "Look closely."

"B-b-but," he stuttered, "I thought you were an angel or—" The girl stood taller and proudly said, "Oh no! I am fully human. I had a father and a mother just like you or any other *human*. There are angels here, but I am *human*, not an angel." The way she said *human* disturbed him a bit. It was as if there was something about being human he was missing. *Maybe that wasn't it exactly,* he thought, *but she doesn't strike me as the average human.* "Forgive me," he stammered, feeling awkward, "but it's hard for me to tell if you are a boy or a girl or a lady or—certainly you must understand that the first thing a doctor has to know about his patient is his or her sex, right?" Though he had been thinking of her as feminine, it had only been a guess.

"Forgive you? Is that a polite but meaningless phrase, or is it a prayer? I mean, you don't seem to be the kind of person who is very familiar with the business of forgiveness."

He was again indignant; but then he couldn't remember off the top of his head, so to speak, of any recent exchange that required forgiveness on his part. *She really has no right to judge me one way or the other.* He spoke his mind, "You're right. I'm not the type. I am not easily offended, and I don't offend others either."

She was pensive. He seemed so relentlessly proud. "I wonder how it feels to be forgiven or even to forgive," she said so quietly that he barely heard her. She lightened somewhat. "Back to me, coming back to whether I am a boy or girl. I am a girl, of course. A fully human girl! Remember, I told you my name, Carlee."

Though he only wanted to think it, he blurted out, "What is with the human thing? If you are a girl, then aren't you human? What else could you be?" He was getting irritated with her and with the direction the conversation was headed.

"That was an excellent question you just asked me, Doctor," she said tentatively. "What else could I be other than a human being?"

"You still haven't told me how I can help you," he demanded, trying to divert her away from the "human" business. "By the way, are we on some kind of timeline here, or does being off the clock mean we could do this forever?"

"Oh no," she answered, "we definitely will not be here forever. When it's time for you to pass through, you will know."

That almost sounded like a threat, and he didn't care for it one bit. In fact, so far, he hadn't experienced anything he would call positive or, in the least, reassuring. Even the presence of this girl person was beginning to make him uneasy.

"Now, as to how you can help me." Carlee put her hands behind her back and leaned into him. He felt an inclination to back up, but how would he do that? he wondered. Even if he wanted to run, he felt that his nonbody state could do nothing but remain in place. He, indeed, was a captive audience for this girl human. "You haven't told me if you remember me," she reminded him. "You thought I was an angel, but since I am not, I must have some connection with you somewhere since I know you. Do you remember me?" she asked again expectantly. "Look carefully."

He saw her clear eyes, flawless skin, brown hair, and lithe figure—pretty and yet not beautiful. Somehow she looked timeless, ageless. Nothing jumped out at him. "Carlee," he repeated almost to himself, studied her face again, and finally replied, "No, I am sorry to say I don't know who you are. Perhaps you could give me a few clues, jog my memory. Don't people change a lot when they get up here, wherever we are? And speaking of where we are, where are we? I would have expected some kind of landscape. Even the moon has a landscape. This light nothingness is boring. If anyone asked me, I'd say it's boring."

Carlee answered apologetically, "I'm sorry. I didn't tell you about the gulf, did I?"

"Gulf of what?" he asked with a mocking tone.

"This is not a gulf of anything, as you might think of a gulf." She paused. "It's a place between. I don't come here often, only to talk to, uh, others who don't immediately enter their final destination. This light nothingness, as you call it, is a sort of a halo or edge of the true light. You would not be able to bear his brightness, and what seems very light to you is somewhat darkened to me in this place. As I tried to explain to you earlier, this is a mere interlude for you, a space between what happened down there"—her eyes glanced down briefly—"and the next part of your journey, which is your time with the Father."

"Oh, honestly," he barked, "you sound like some kind of mystic. You're talking in a language I don't understand. Frankly, I feel like you are wasting my time. Oh yes, I forgot. Time is a non-issue here." All he needed to know was his whereabouts. Was that too much to ask? If he was really dead, this was no time for mysteries! His frustration was growing.

"You asked, Doctor, and I was trying to explain as simply as I could where you are. Your impatience or boredom, as you call it, has no bearing on our time together, so perhaps we should move on."

He felt chastised, an unfamiliar and very distasteful sensation. If he had chains wrapped around his hands and feet, which he remembered as being absent, he couldn't feel more a prisoner than he felt now. He also began to fret about not knowing her and grew more indignant that she expected him to remember her out of all the people who had passed through his office doors over the past twenty years. He reminded her of the scope of his practice and that it was unrealistic for her to expect he would know her.

She barely acknowledged his defense as to why he couldn't remember her. "Yes," she answered, "I have changed since last we met, and well, our visit was so short. I don't think you took a really good look at me before you—and after it was over, I seemed less myself. In fact, myself never came into being. I didn't get to know myself, you know, in a human kind of way."

Chapter 4

In a patronizing tone, he responded, "Now you sound silly. You sound like you've gone off the deep end. Were you suffering from depression or some kind of psychiatric disorder? That wasn't my specialty, you know." Obviously, the girl had taken leave of her mind, poor thing, and now he was supposed to help her through some personal identity crisis! He was in no frame of mind to provide counseling. That seemed fairly obvious.

Apologetically, Carlee admitted that perhaps she had not been fair with him. "I have waited such a long time for this meeting with you, and I guess it is harder than I thought it would be. I will be more straightforward with you."

"Finally!" He blurted, "But by all means, take your time, Carol. Evidently, time is something I have a lot of now."

"Carlee, not Carol," the girl corrected.

"Carlee then," he quipped. "Can we get to the point now that we are clear on names?"

She tilted her head down slightly and in barely more than a whisper said slowly and deliberately, "You took me from my mother before I was born. I went past you through a suction tube, into the city sewer in little pieces. How could I expect you to recognize me, but certainly you remember, don't you?"

Now he was disgusted. He defended, "Does that damnable debate go on here too? I thought it was settled long ago. The fetus is a nonperson, at most, a potential human, an appendix of sorts that has no meaning until after it is fully developed and born." He went on, "There were even some who contended that until a child can care for itself by even the most primitive means, it is not entitled to life as a human. It could be eliminated quite late if the practitioner deemed it necessary. Of course, I never would have followed through on that extreme notion. I, compared to many of my colleagues, was very conservative. I never liked to abort after eight to ten weeks. I didn't care about identifying sex and features. It served no purpose whatsoever. If I identified nothing, then I had nothing to report. Some women, girls, had questions about the, uh, product of conception. I told them what I saw: a coagulation of cells with no identity that I could determine. Once they were removed from the mother's body and drawn up into the tubing, there was little to recognize, really," he added, sounding a bit less confident and even defensive as he continued, "If we really believed the product of conception is a human in its beginning, would we have terminated it? Really, Carlee, think about it. I did only what the law allowed, and besides, it was your mother's choice. I simply complied with her request. You cannot blame me. I will not stand here and listen to an accusation that makes me look like a criminal." His defense fell short. Even he could see that. He was standing. At least in his mind, he was standing on his non-legs before a human being, clearly nothing more or less than a perfectly normal, though somewhat uncommon, human being.

"Dr. Boresman, you have avoided the issue. In the choice debate, you have to admit you weren't sure if we were human or not, but you chose. You chose to believe we were not, so the question was not settled, only the choice. Did you not close your mind and turn a blind eye to the truth you learned in your study of human reproduction, the joining of two cells, multiplication of those cells resulting in a heart and lungs, kidneys, fingers, toes, all with their own unique cell identity? What did you think would come from that union: a mouse, a kitten, or perhaps a monkey?" She stopped. This was not for her to do.

"So"—he let out a mirthless laugh—"this is judgment day. Now you get your revenge. Is this what this is all about, some kind of hell because I perform perfectly legal abortions?" That fear—no, not fear—terror was seeping back into his consciousness.

"No, no," Carlee pleaded, "not revenge. This is not about revenge. I am certainly not your judge. That privilege is reserved for the Only Qualified One. Remember, I told you our meeting is not about you but about me. "He is allowing me to spend time with you to study you as a human being, to glean from you emotion and motive. When I was wrenched from my mother, I came here, and I suppose you were right to imagine I am an angel. I have never experienced anything human, and perhaps I was spared some dreadful life, but I will never know that. I missed being a part of a family, going to school, falling in love, marrying, perhaps having children of my own. I missed out on a full emotional life, you know, all the experiences, both good and bad, that contribute to people and make them into what they are and who they become during their lifetimes. I suppose you could say, sir, that I never had the chance to choose. Now please, Doctor, you must understand that I am not complaining. I am in the tender care of the One whose love is the only burden I have ever borne, and I am completely satisfied. You know, it has been said that angels long to look into the affairs of men, to try to understand redemption, and so I guess I am like an angel in that sense. I long to understand the business of being human since that was my beginning, being human. Remember, that is why we are here. I am having an opportunity to explore for myself. Isn't that what humans do?"

Desperate now to end this nonsense, the man asked, "What then, are we going to continue this debate until I am convinced you are right and then you will be satisfied?"

"Oh no, debate is an exercise of the intellect. To debate is to convince someone of truth or perhaps nontruth. The reason we are allowed this time is not the debate but feelings themselves, emotions, a wonder that is so unappreciated by humanity. You were in a world created in such a way that you could respond to it, to know feelings of joy or sadness, to be awed by beauty or repudiated by ugliness. The privilege was and is so taken for granted that the idea of being thankful for an emotional life never seems to occur to so many. Wouldn't you say that emotional experiences are sought after, sometimes at the expense of morality and right choices, though?"

Impatiently, he retorted, "You are putting way too much emphasis on feelings. I don't understand."

"You don't understand because feelings were so much a part of who you are, uh, were. Knowing what you know now, imagine having never experienced the world that allowed you to weep, to dance, to soar, to love, to work, even to hate and feel failure, a world filled with challenges to overcome. You can't, can you? Humans were made for all that, but we who were 'terminated' were simply dismissed. We never existed except as an inconvenience or an interruption or a 'thing' that had to be dealt with, hidden until the time at which we would be eliminated. No one would ever have to know our potentiality, our existence as a member of the human race while we were growing and changing, moment by moment, in what should have been a safe place."

Chapter 5

This was getting to be too much. *She is trying to elicit some guilt in me,* he thought, *some feeling of remorse. Feeling*—there was that word. He began to speak but was overwhelmed with a memory of his wife, his children. How could he have forgotten? What were they thinking right now? Did they know about—as quickly as the thoughts came, they vanished. "We were never certain," he responded. "How many times do I have to tell you that? I did what I believed was the best thing to do for women who came to me with desperate situations. I helped. That was my calling, to help."

Carlee tilted her head to one side and closed her eyes for a moment as if thinking what to say next. "Ah," she said quietly, "all that you needed to make right decisions was available to you. The obvious truth was creation and a Creator. He spoke through what he had made, through history, through his Word. He sent a spokesman who made the way to himself accessible for everyone, and he simply longed to be heard, to be believed. How could you conclude at any point in your life that he would plan conception, guide the development of tiny cells in a very complicated and yet safe environment, and then call it less than human life in the case of humans, of course? How could you possibly believe that he would give you permission to destroy what he began?"

The doctor was becoming exceedingly frustrated, but he couldn't strike out at this girl or run from her. He demanded, "Then you are continuing this debate. We will argue it until what? You said that this is about you. Then get to the point! I am weary of circling the same old wagon."

Carlee agreed. "You are here to help me understand what you were thinking, what brought you to the point of taking a human life and feeling nothing. There are so many of us here, a whole unique culture of sorts. As I said before, we are not angels or products of human experience such as you are, for instance. You have forty-seven years of living that have contributed to all that you have become. Even a young baby, who is born alive and then dies, has had a taste, be it ever so limited, of humanness: the love of a mother, sights, and sounds. Many seemingly insignificant experiences contributed to his or her brief life. Our lives, and all that God intended us to be, were cut short before they ever began, which leaves us wanting, in a very human sense, I mean."

"God! I should have known that we were going to get to God. You are making an assumption that I believe in God in the first place, at least in the sense that you do," he interrupted.

She went on as if he had not spoken, "Please understand, Doctor, as we go through this process that I, along with all those aborted ones, lack nothing. I cannot make you understand the totality of contentment, love, nourishment, perfect peace that we experience every day. Umm, really there are no days and nights here, but for the sake of your scope of understanding, relative to time, we will say days. That, of course, will change for you once you pass on from here." Her eyes moved away from him, looking somewhere far away. He rebelled at the notion that she knew something he did not, and angrily he shouted, "Get on with it! Spare me the lecture on time or lack of it!"

She continued, completely unruffled by him, "The Father has granted me, for a moment, access to as much information as I can glean from the human experience as it relates to me. Obviously my contacts are few and short-lived: my parents who gave me life and you, who took it. You might say I am finding my roots."

He all but snorted, "This sounds like some kind of celestial voyeurism to me. You mean you are spying on and invading the private lives of unsuspecting people? Call me foolish, if you will, but that is an invasion of people's right to privacy, and that, I should point out, is no small deal where I come from."

"I suppose if I were using the information for personal gain or some selfish or criminal purpose, you could argue that, but I assure you, I am not. It is not the intimate details of a human life that I explore but rather the sensations, the feelings, as I said before, that make a human what he or she is, what influences the decision-making process, which is so profoundly different from animals, and their response to their environment since they function only at the level of instinct. For instance, think of the eye, formed to behold subtleties of colors splashed on the ocean as the sun drops below the horizon or what of the physics of the human ear that allows it to receive certain impulses, which are transported to the brain and then translated as music or voice or rain falling. Even pain experienced when something hot is touched is converted to a response, and you pull away from the causative source—and, oh, so much more. These sensations are unique to humankind, a gift, not just life but abundant life! All this you took for granted. But as the result of what you call choice, I have missed out completely, and so I study and learn and vicariously make as much of it as is possible my own. Now again, I know I am speaking outside of anything that is rational to you. I am simply asking you to bear with me."

"As if I have any choice in the matter," he responded, feeling less and less himself as the time passed. *Choice*—now there was a word he was beginning to hate. "I still think you are on a rabbit trail of revenge and you aren't willing to admit it. And as for the Father allowing it all, I can't say much for his good judgment."

Chapter 6

Carlee did not defend the accusation of revenge or the doctor's assessment of the Father's judgment. He could not fully understand the nature of their discussion, and his only point of reference is still himself, so very self-absorbed.

"What of your family, Dr. Boresman? Tell me something about your family."

He softened for a moment and thought about Jennifer, his beautiful wife, and Michael and Megan, his children, both in college, successful, and focused. In his mind's eye, he saw them so clearly that they seemed almost reachable. "My family has been everything to me. All that I did was for them. My wife has not had to work. She does volunteer work at a retirement center, plays tennis, has dinner parties. She's an angel, well, nearly," he added. "My children graduated from high school with honors and have no financial concerns. They adore me and I, them."

"My"—he paused, searching for the word—"passing is going to devastate them." His tone became desperate. "Is there no way to contact them, to let them know that I am—"

Carlee could hear the pain in his voice, but she had no comforting words. "No one ever goes back from here, Doctor, contrary to what some have said. There is no reunion, except, of course, for those who carry no burdens with them. They will be united with their loved ones again."

Suddenly the man felt great loss, greater than the loss of his own life. He let out a wail of grief, "I don't deserve this! My family doesn't deserve this! We are good and decent people!" He focused on Carlee. "You can do something to change this. I am sorry that I aborted you, and I will apologize to all those others. I couldn't possibly have known that I would be held accountable. It was not my fault. Don't you understand that the times and culture dictate right from wrong?" There was no sorrow accompanying his outburst, no real apology. He knew it. He was throwing out words that he thought she wanted to hear, words he hoped might change the direction in which he was headed. A sense of hopelessness was gaining on him, though, and he knew that too.

"No, I do not understand," she replied. "Remember, I never had the chance to live out my life. I can only suppose from this perfect place, and knowing the Author of Life and what I have learned from him, that any man or woman with any knowledge would know the difference between right and wrong, life and death. Strictly from my perspective, that seems very straightforward, no middle ground. You see, this is the struggle. How could you take life that you did not know or had any feelings for one way or another? It wasn't as if you were at war and we were the enemy. Could you not have said no? There are some here who were nearly born, and at the last possible moment, just an instant before a breath could be taken, they were terminated. There are some who were, or so the abortionist thought, killed in the womb with chemicals and then delivered from their mothers. Some of those did not die until they smothered in a lidded box, which sat waiting to receive their little bodies, mean coffins, wouldn't you say? But you know all this. You are in a sense a co-inventor of the horror. I am not vengeful, as I said before, because that's not my place, but I am confused. There is a disconnect. It is almost as if a truth and a lie are standing side by side and make a vow to wed, but try as they may, they cannot touch each other because an invisible barrier stands between them. Because a procedure was declared legal, how did that make it ethical? With legality at the forefront, ethics slid under the carpet and were never heard from again except by those who did and do discern right from wrong, life and death. Their voices are drowned out by the drumbeat of choice."

"You see, you see," the man stuttered, "this debate continues. I want it to be done, and you want it to go on. I will remain convinced forever that I did what made sense to me, and you will tell me that I believed a lie, or are you insinuating that I am a liar and, worse yet, a lie? I am an intelligent man. I can stand my ground in any argument. I have a wall covered with framed degrees. I have spent half of my life studying. I am no fool!"

Carlee pushed a strand of her light-brown hair away from her face and asked, "What of Michael and Megan? What if all that you know about them and love in them never really existed? Let's say that your wife's pregnancy was poorly timed, and you were not in a position to support a family. So you decided to abort Michael, at least, because he came first and his insinuation into your lives was an inconvenience. Which part of his life would have ever been insignificant even while he grew in the safety of Jennifer's womb, the result of your loving relationship with her? At which point in that experience would you have been willing to terminate him: when you first learned of conception, the first movement, the first time you felt him kick, or just before he entered the world? Was his full potential as a man encased in those few cells or not? What if you had aborted him, dismissed him before he was born? At which point when you knew that Jennifer was pregnant did you believe she was potentially carrying anything less than a human being?"

"That is not fair!" he shouted, "That is not fair! They were wanted and planned, and I would kill *for* them!"

"Indeed a most excellent argument, Dr. Boresman, because that is precisely why I stand before you—unwanted, unplanned, and therefore killed—and any gain you received from my death supported your own offspring. And I struggle to see the fairness." She was not angry, but a hint of passion colored her words. She was simply stating facts.

He wondered how she could be so self-controlled.

Chapter 7

Suddenly, it seemed to the doctor that he was moving toward an even brighter light. It took him off guard, and he asked the girl, "What is going on here?"

She answered, "Our time is almost finished here, and you will have to go. I need to ask you one more thing. My mother—do you remember her? Her name is Melanie. She was only sixteen when you met her, just a girl herself. She spent a few minutes with you before you performed the procedure. You didn't even ask her what her circumstances were. She was alone and wept through the whole thing, and you chatted with your nurse about a football game you were going to take your son to on the weekend. Do you remember Melanie? She paid you cash."

The man laughed. "Do you have any idea how many patients I have treated? Certainly you are joking me when you ask if I remember your mother. Very few went through the, uh, procedure without shedding a few tears. It was not painless, you know—"

"I know it was not painless. Remember, I was there too, Dr. Boresman," Carlee interjected before he was finished. A long and uncomfortable silence rested between them when he grasped her meaning.

"Didn't I say I was sorry? You see, this is simply the debate in the disguise of some philosophical exploration. I am being used in your search for emotional connection, and somehow that does not seem quite fair to me. I am dead. Shouldn't I be allowed to get on with the business of being dead, whatever that is?"

"Soon enough, you will get on with it. We are almost finished." Carlee paused, gazing so deeply into him that he felt transparent, which he remembered that he actually was. "I want you to know that you have contributed a great deal to me, and I am appreciative. Before we part, I will tell you exactly how you have helped, but I wanted you to know some things about my mother, Melanie. I am sorry you don't remember her because she really is a lovely person. She did finish school and get married. She had three more children, but there's not a day in her life that she doesn't look at them and think about me. Of course, she never knew if I was a boy or a girl, but she knew I was human, and the burden she carries is far greater than if she had borne me. She has since learned that there were people who could have helped her. There were alternatives to abortion, but from her perspective, she did what she thought was her only choice. Doesn't that seem strange to you, Doctor, to call abortion a choice if you are never given the other options so as to make a legitimate choice? The counselor in your clinic told her that in a few minutes, her troubles would be over. She could move on with her life without an unwanted burden. And no one would ever have to know. Had she talked to her about adoption or going through with her pregnancy, then she could have chosen. As difficult as it might have been, she could have had a choice. My mother has been forgiven. She found a friend shortly after who helped her to find the Father. Someday we will meet, and all her sadness will be gone forever."

Chapter 8

Dr. Boresman was beginning to feel terribly beaten, weary; this conversation had gone on long enough. She was getting her revenge, and frankly, he didn't care. *Let her have it! All of them—let them come and get me.* "Will there be more of you coming after me?" he asked with resignation. "A parade of aborted children to torture me with their accusations? I have no regrets, though you have done your best to make me say that I have. The only regret I have is that I didn't see that truck coming. I think it was a truck," he said almost to himself, "and my family and all that money I put in my 401(k). I wish I could have spent more of it. My wife, Jennifer—I'm having trouble remembering what she looks like just now." The sharpness of his good memories was fading. In fact, even his bad memories were hard for him to pull up. He was so tired. He looked at Carlee and asked, almost pleaded, "What's happening? I'm having trouble holding a thought or a memory." He felt like a child trying to grab hold of his own shadow, completely uncomprehending of the inaccessibility of what seemed to be part of him. The gulf was widening and the light nothingness thickening. He was suffocating or falling or drowning. He couldn't tell which.

Carlee knew what was happening; he was being called away from her. He was going to have to carry the full load of his burdens before the throne. If there only had been some way to convince him, in his lifetime, that his greatest sins were not all that he had committed; it was one, the sin of disbelief, that would reach its long and icy finger into eternity and then slowly but surely settle fully into his consciousness.

He forced himself to connect with her again. "I have really never been afraid of anything, you know, until now. What I fear most is that I won't be able to defend myself. That is really important to me, to be able to stand my ground, to justify myself and my actions. Before God, I have done nothing but what I thought was right." He felt much less confident than he sounded.

The girl—her eyes deep and liquid, like a pool, he thought—responded, "That is the crux of it all, Dr. Boresman, before God! All that you did and did not do was before God whether you believe in him or not. This fear you feel right now will pass, and you will indeed prepare your defense, but you will weary of it soon. The need to defend yourself will slowly become less important, and so will your good memories. The burden, however, will become unbearable. The weight of your sins will be too heavy to carry, and yet you must. I would have forgiven you. In fact, I do forgive you. All of us who died at your hands have forgiven you, but ultimately, it is not us with whom you have to do. As the bigger picture takes shape, you will realize that it was not against us that you sinned. As I said, do you remember? The one sin of disbelief cannot be forgiven. Not now. If only…"

He felt a surge of anger flare in him. "You have no right! You are no one, a child with a grudge! How dare you stand there and tell me about my sins? If you represent God, he is a bitter disappointment to me. What about kindness, light, and—what was that I heard about God? Oh yes, I remember: 'the benevolent, all-loving One who could choose to overlook even the greatest of offenses.' Yes, now it's coming to me. I heard a message on television one night when I couldn't sleep. I was actually tempted to send some money to the man. His eloquence was matched only by the elegance of his suit. I think it was a Marcus Lehman or something, very expensive. I thought better of financing him, however, when I realized that if he could afford a suit of that quality, he didn't need my money. Ah, but I digress." He felt energized somehow by this talk about God. "*The Many Pathways to God* or something like that was a book I read, in fact, just very recently. It all made perfect sense to me that the intellect of man should not be squandered on mindless dribble such as one way. The narrowness of that thinking shrinks our wisdom, making us puppets that have no will at all. Yes, I remember now. The author pictured God sitting on a throne with as many paths leading to him or her as there are systems of religion and people. In fact, he noted that we are all free to develop our own religion, some obviously more complex than others, depending on our intellectual capacity. I was utterly fascinated by the conceptualization of God being taken out of the realm of smallness to infinite largeness. I could really wrap my mind around that kind of god. The human intellect has taken so many strides away from the primitive notions of blind faith in some invisible despot." He stopped to notice if the girl was with him or not. What was he saying? Even to his own ears, his dissertation on God sounded hollow, echoing back at him like a bad string on an out-of-tune piano. Obviously, it fell flat on Carlee. Her eyes were closed, and her head bowed slightly.

She asked, "Do you truly not yet see that the empty ideas and fantasies of human imagination, energized by a lie and *the* liar, do not fit into the economy of the One God? Do you still, even as you stand dead in your own sins, not believe that there is an accountability to which you must be held? Choice, Doctor. You had the opportunity to make the one choice that mattered, but you were so distracted by other issues, and then there was that matter of choice that took you further and further away from any hope of redemption. I do believe that you knew. Every time you encountered a woman with a life growing in her, you knew that it was wrong to rip it out of her. You had lots of support, though, didn't you? The government, your friends, your family, most members of your profession—they all believed the lie: out of sight, out of mind. I think that early on you hoped your choices wouldn't come back to haunt you, didn't you? But then, you pushed that uncomfortable thought as far back in your mind as you could."

He began to answer her, but suddenly he lost his train of thought. *Wasn't I just on the precipice of discovery, a remembrance of some piece of wisdom?* "What was the question?" he asked. A fog was dropping over his mind, and he felt a compulsion to go. *Go where?* he thought. *I don't have any means to leave, and I have no directions.* Carlee was still with him. He tried to clear his mind, to focus. "Carlee!"

"Yes," she answered, "I am here."

"I can't remember the question you asked a moment ago."

She sighed. "The question doesn't matter now, Doctor. What does matter, however, is that we finish what we started. I told you that this encounter was about me and not you. Soon you will have forgotten our time together as you move on to your eternal work, bearing the burdens you could have shed."

She was making no sense to him now. Of course, he would remember her and all that they had talked about. He certainly would not forget the debate because, evidently, he was going to have to defend himself again in this place. *Of course, I was right, and I have to hang on to that truth. The law is on my side*, he reasoned with himself. For a moment, he forgot the girl was there. He began composing a defense in his mind; but when he began to plan it out, he couldn't make two thoughts stick together. Frustrated, he comforted himself with the idea that this was going to be a test, an exam of sorts. Cramming would not help him, but all his study and work and his innate intelligence would pay off at the last minute. *Don't worry, Paul, you'll be fine, once you get over this little hurdle.* Suddenly he said to Carlee, "A hurdle—that's what you are, a hurdle, one that I have to get over in order to move on! I should have known. I should have been more compassionate to you, more understanding of your situation. I was so frightened and confused there for a bit. I forgot my oath, my commitment to keep my patient's best interest always before me. There! I hope I have not failed you, young lady. You must understand that the whole accident business and finding myself without a body threw me for a loop, but I think I'm getting it now. I really should have had a longer adjustment period, you know, a few explanations of what was ahead before we jumped right into your problems." He felt somewhat relieved, certain now that he was going to get control of this circumstance. He just needed to play along, make the girl believe that perhaps she is right. *It won't hurt me to let her think she has convinced me that I was wrong*, he plotted. *She has said a lot of harsh things, though, about my life's work. She's trying to make me feel guilty, and if I give in here, it will make any defense I have to make further along even more of a challenge.*

Chapter 9

"Doctor? Dr. Boresman?" Carlee called.

"Yes, yes, of course, I'm here. I was just mulling over all that we have debated here, and I should say that I think you believe that you are completely right, and I need to respect that. Forgive me for trying to convince you otherwise. I was being very inconsiderate. I can see where you might have felt robbed, so to speak, of life, but there is another side to that coin, Carlee. Have you ever considered that your removal out of an extremely stressful circumstance gave another person—your mother, for instance—the freedom to go on with the pursuit of her own life goals? You can think of it as a sacrifice that you made for her sake. As I recall, sacrifice is a very big deal here. Are you following me?" he asked.

The girl lifted her hand and commanded with firmness, "Stop now! You are stepping over a line that you simply cannot cross. You know nothing of sacrifice, especially the sacrifice that was conceived and born in this place. If you did, we would not be having this discussion. Your burdens, the weight of which you have not yet begun to feel, could all have been left at the feet of him who sacrificed his very life for you!"

"There indeed is another side to the coin, actually more of a triangle than a coin: my father. He passed through here not too much longer after I did. He was a very troubled person, very careless you might say. He was careless with my mother. In fact, everything he touched he left broken." The doctor thought he perceived moistness in Carlee's eyes he had not noticed before. "He didn't even know that I existed. Melanie, my mother, was used and discarded, and he, when I asked him, he couldn't even remember her name. He had no interest in talking to me, and so it seemed pointless for me to press him, so he moved on rather quickly." She was thoughtful. "He was surly, unconcerned, and more than eager to carry his own load. Evidently, no one in his life had ever held him accountable. He didn't know that his free spirit would soon be held captive forever. The knee he had never bent would bend but not freely." The girl was making no sense to the doctor now, and his intellectual prowess was struggling to formulate some response, but anything he could think of to say was nonsense, even to his own ears. *Where was she going with all this? Oh yes, her father.*

He attempted to comfort her, "That must have been very hard on your self-esteem when he told you that he didn't know anything about you. I can understand how that must have made you feel. Rejection is very painful, I suppose, at almost any level."

"Yes, at almost any level, Doctor," she reminded him sadly. "However, you are mistaken to think that I pity myself. Oh no! Remember how I explained that I am whole and healed. I am not pitiable, but rather I pity. I am grieving for my father, for he is much to be pitied, much as I pity you. His loss is immeasurable, not because he didn't know *me* but because he didn't know his Heavenly Father. Soon, very soon, all the sadness we feel for those lost will be taken away. God will clear up forever our misunderstandings about human nature and the power it has in the decision-making process. We will see all the human responses not in a glass darkly, but in perfect clarity from the One who gives perfect reason. The Word will speak, and we will see the truth through him. You might say we will at last comprehend the mind of God in some small and yet infinitely significant way, the way in which God intended humanity to know him from the beginning. We turned off the light, not him. We loved the darkness, thinking we knew best. I say *we* because even though I had no opportunity to make life choices, I still bear the stamp of my first parents and their wrong choices. The Son is Light, Dr. Boresman, and so even the foulest of deeds are committed in his sight, exposed. So as much as humans try to shut him out, they cannot any more than they can turn off the sun."

He was weary of the girl's sermonizing. "If you are trying to convince me of your point of view because it will somehow vindicate you or produce something in me that will make me more acceptable, you are wasting your time. Although you did mention time was no object here, I am tired. Have you gained from me what you had hoped? Has your use of me satisfied your need for connection? I certainly hope so! One thing puzzles me, though. What you deem as a privilege, being human, is not all that great, really. Wars, calamity, disease, waste, inhuman acts committed against one another, all kinds of suffering sometimes outweigh the good things in life. For instance, for a few years, I enjoyed a very sheltered life. Aside from a few financial struggles, I haven't actually had as many difficulties as many people I know. But…here I am. It's over. What is the advantage of the human experience if you can bypass it and still enjoy, uh, whatever it is that you enjoy here? You said to me that you are completely satisfied. All those people whose lives were interrupted, as you have put it, haven't had any choice, but choice can be a two-edged sword, you know. Human beings, by and large, are more likely to make bad decisions as they are to make good ones. Then what? Isn't it better for them to *not* have had the opportunity to choose wrongly?"

"Dear, Doctor, you have missed my point entirely," Carley answered. "Because you, your family and those around you have all been making choices. You haven't given the whole notion much thought, except, of course, choice as it pertains to me and our discussion here. Your wife, Jennifer, for instance, can choose where to live, what to eat, what kind of car to drive, the clothing she will wear, what she will do with her day. Needless to say, many, probably most people on the planet, do not enjoy the freedom of choices that she does in your particular culture, but that is not my point here. The crux of the matter is, why would you—I am speaking of the larger you—dub the killing of an unborn child as a woman's right to choose when she is, in fact, faced with myriads of choices every day and the freedom to do whatever she chooses? The idea of choices has never even occurred to a woman in this day and age. And yet, Melanie, my mother, was not given choices in the matter of her unborn child—me, specifically—as I said before. She thought there was only one way out of her dilemma when, in fact, there were other choices she could have made were she given all the facts. I am suggesting that prochoice has nothing to do with choice at all. It is simply a matter of taking a life that is inconvenient. Had it been called prodeath, 100 percent fatal, which is exactly what it is, for the unborn, anyway, perhaps fewer would have taken that road. A naked error, murder, is a very ugly, repugnant act. How much better to dress it up in some elegant cover, like prochoice, and then the unwary find it palatable, even more true than the truth itself."

Utter exhaustion rolled over him like a rogue wave, overwhelming him completely.

The doctor sighed. "Carlee, Carlee, you say we are not debating, but you are, and it is finished because I have resolved that we will have to agree to disagree. Why do you go on and on as if to convince me of your point of view? You have said yourself that it is too late. The die has been cast, so to speak. Even if I had a sudden change of heart and agreed with you that abortion is a crime, what difference would it make now? All the deeds have been done. I can't undo anything. Isn't that what you have said? It's over for me?" His own words stung him, the words *too late*. They were so final, so hopeless. It occurred to him that what was too late for him was not just losing out on a good buy or missing a plane but simply losing out altogether. He was dead, after all. *Dead, dead, ugly word, dead,* he mused. As one who presses the worst memory of one's life down to the depths of his mind, hoping it never resurfaces, he moved away from the word. The girl was staring at him as if he was an alien. Now that he thought of it, he wondered what she was seeing. Was it his bare, naked soul? What did it look like? he wondered. Before he was taken away or whatever was to happen to him, he had to finish this. "Have you learned anything from me that will help you connect to your human roots? Isn't that what you wanted from me?"

She stood, hands at her side, still looking at him with profound intensity; and there was something else that he struggled to define in her look: love perhaps, not love as he had ever known it but a love mixed with compassion and tenderness and…forgiveness. She was so wise and lovely and innocent. He suddenly wished he'd known her under different circumstances. His mind was clouding. A storm was brewing, and he couldn't control it. He felt an unexpected, unwanted, and certain cataclysmic jolt as he continued to look at her, fearful of losing the only shred of human contact left for him. She seemed to be losing substance, or was the light absorbing her? She was saying something; but though he strained to hear her, he could not make out the words. Urgency struck him; and before she left him utterly alone, he had to say something to her. Everything was different now. They hadn't finished, but he was spent: exhausted, sick of himself, really. Tired of listening to his own voice and wearied by his useless defense. How does a man live his entire life under the wings of the obvious and miss it? She had asked him that question, and he had no answer. Actually he knew the answer, but he wouldn't say it. To go against the tide would have been too costly, and he never thought much about the future, except to keep his 401(k) growing—early retirement, all the perks that come with being on the top. He had never thought about this scenario. Why would he? And now. For the first time in his life, he felt sorrow. All the pride he felt when he had told Carlee he had neither been offended or nor offended settled on what was left of his brain like acid. Now when it was too late, he knew that he had offended not one but thousands. Two words left his mouth, two words he couldn't ever remember saying in his entire life, at least not in the way he was saying them now: "Forgive me."

Chapter 10

He thought he heard his name, but it was so faint that he couldn't be certain. The blanket of light was so bright that it nearly blinded him. He looked for Carlee, called her name, but she was gone. Had she heard him ask for forgiveness? Suddenly that mattered more than anything else, but the place where she had stood was empty. There it was again: "Paul." He heard it more clearly this time. He was desperate to get to the voice, though he suspected it was judgment time. He didn't care. "Carlee!" he called. "Carlee!"

The person calling him was beginning to sound desperate, "Paul, Paul, can you hear me? Squeeze my hand if you can hear me!" How ridiculous those words sounded to him. *I have no hands with which to squeeze. I have no body, in fact.* He wanted to shout back, but what was the point? It occurred to him that this was another of the hurdles he would have to get over, Carlee being the first. Carlee, he suddenly remembered, had not told him how he had helped her. Their conversation had ended so abruptly because of the voice, and yet she was so determined to find a connection with him that would bring her some measure of completion. He tried to remember her last words, but they weren't coming to him. He only remembered his own: "Forgive me." He recalled the vast all-encompassing feeling of sadness that had overcome him just before he had let the words slip out of his mouth.

"Paul, Paul, hey, Paul, can you hear me?" There was that voice again. Even though there was an extreme sense of urgency about the man's voice, and he really wanted to respond, he couldn't; he was too far away. He had to think about what it was that caused him to feel sorry. It wasn't really Carlee. She had rejected the idea that he should pity her; this was something else with which he needed to come to grips.

Chapter 11

He was adrift now. The light was getting brighter. It was hurting his eyes; and though he willed to shut the light out, it felt like someone was holding his eyes open, forcing him to look at it. Strange and yet vaguely familiar noises assaulted his senses, but they were out of place in the gulf—beeps and sighs, rhythmic and constant. He tried to reorient himself to the gulf, but now it was different. The light was intense but focal, not surrounding him as it had. With an awareness that sent shockwaves through him, he realized that he wasn't in the gulf anymore. Everything had changed; he had a body! He knew it because of the severe pain, terrible pain in his chest and arms and back. Muffled voices surrounded him. Someone was whispering and then, "Paul, Paul! Are you with me, Paul?" It was a man's voice, no one that he recognized.

Of course I can hear you, but I'm suffocating. Can't you see that? He wanted to scream but couldn't. He struggled against the weight pressing down on his chest. He had to free himself! He had to escape from the pain, or he would go mad. There was a woman's voice asking a question of someone, an answer, and then a flood; a flood of relief began to sweep over him. It coursed through him, soothing, calming. It was taking him away from the pain. He was floating away, and he stopped struggling. The light was still over him, but it was softer now. The noises, the sound of dripping water—they were all fading. He decided to wait for Carlee to find him, and then they could continue; but even her visage that had been so clear to him moments ago, moments before he had been pulled away to suffocation and pain, was foggy, indistinct, and gone. Who was she anyway? Dr. Boresman slept a dreamless sleep. The last thought that passed through his mind was "Another hurdle."

Slowly the doctor was being pulled up out of blessed unconsciousness by a very pressing matter; he was in a freefall. From where to where he couldn't tell, but he couldn't stop it. A voice, again unfamiliar, was pleading with him to relax, "Paul, you're okay. We have you. We aren't going to let you fall. We are just changing your position, turning you onto your side." He felt a tight grip on his arms and legs and another pair of hands on his head, and he was indeed turning. *The pain, oh my god, the pain.* He felt hot tears involuntarily well in his eyes and spill down his cheeks. The moisture made his face itch, and he automatically tried to lift his right hand to scratch, but it wouldn't budge. The effort caused him so much discomfort that in desperation he tried his left hand, but someone was pressing it into the bed. Then he felt the tug of a restraint securing his hand to something. He was completely powerless and in so much pain. He heard a soft whisper at his right ear, a voice he knew instantly, "Paul, honey, try to relax. The nurse is going to give you some more medicine to take the pain away."

"Jennifer, Jennifer!" he silently cried. "Jennifer, I'm not dead, and I have so much to tell you!" He tried to open his eyes, but they felt glued shut; and before he could continue the effort, he felt a burning in his arm, but it soon turned to warmth. Then he was awash in waves of relief, so he let the drugs do their work. The beeps, the pulsating throbs, the sighs of the state-of-the-art medical equipment that were, for now, sustaining his life lulled him; and he drifted away.

Chapter 12

What Paul Boresman did not know is that he had been in this hospital bed for four days, his life all the while hanging in the balance. It was nothing short of a miracle that he was not killed outright in the accident. Had it taken the medical crew even another two minutes to pry his body out of the little car, he would have certainly died at the scene. As it was, he had a skull fracture, five broken ribs, a compound fracture of his right arm, damage to his left kidney, and fractures of both legs. Both of his eyes had sustained injuries when the airbag slammed his sunglasses into them. The extent of damage was yet unknown. If he could have seen himself lying there, he would have been shocked. For all intents and purposes, he should have been dead; and perhaps, for a time, he had been. He had been in a drug-induced coma to allow the machines to sustain his life until he could do the work of breathing—or not.

From Jennifer's perspective, the whole scenario was nothing less than terrifying. There was nothing about the man lying in the bed that looked like her husband, Paul. His face was terribly bloated and bruised; his eyes were taped shut to keep the swollen tissues from drying out. Both legs and his right arm were splinted, and bloody drainage seeped through the dressings. His entire body, where there was not a dressing or a splint, was black-and-blue and fluid filled. She was told that the fractured ribs would be the hardest to deal with because of the pain he would have breathing deeply enough on his own to provide adequate oxygenation. The doctors had further frightened her with the cold, hard fact that he was not out of the woods yet. His recovery could be complicated by blood clots to his lungs, infections, and organ failure. She heard the words, but their meaning was going unprocessed.

She needed hope; she was not prepared to accept anything less than the promise that he was going to be fine.

Jennifer slipped into her husband's room in the ICU and sat tentatively on the edge of the recliner at her husband's bedside, her hands in her lap. She watched the nurse on the opposite side of the bed turning dials, checking the monitor, emptying tubes, readjusting the sheet covering her broken husband and the pillows that supported his limbs. The name tag that dangled on the lanyard around the nurse's neck was flipped so that her name was not visible. Jennifer looked at the white board on the wall where the nurse had written the date, doctor of the day, and other pertinent information. While she studied the board, the nurse came alongside of her and introduced herself, "Mrs. Boresman, I am Carlee, your husband's nurse today. I was here the day your husband was admitted, but I doubt you would remember me, and that is fine. I will be here for the next twelve hours, and if there is anything I can do for you, please ask. The report this morning was quite good. Dr. Boresman had an uneventful night and actually required less pain medication and sedation than he has previously needed. We are waiting for the results of bloodwork done this morning. I know that you must be exhausted. Can I get you a cup of coffee or tea?" Jennifer nodded gratefully. "Coffee. Black, please. Thank you." Carlee was back with the coffee in a few minutes and placed it along with some graham crackers on a bedside table. The nurse then pulled up a chair and sat across from the woman.

"Do you have any questions I can answer or concerns that I can address for you?" Her warm smile and gentle manner immediately put Jennifer at ease. She continued, "I know that you have been with your husband every day since his accident, and I know too that you have had lots of discussions with his doctors, but sometimes things occur to you after the fact, after the doctor has left the room".

Jennifer nodded and agreed out loud that the physicians sometimes seemed hurried, and she didn't want to take up any more of their time than they were already giving. "I guess the one question I have is the one that no one wants to answer. Is he going to be all right?"

The nurse placed her hand on Jennifer's arm and quietly said, "I know. I can tell you that I am encouraged by the fact that Dr.

Boresman has had no setbacks, and from what I have seen, he seems to be improving every day." She glanced over at the man in the bed and added, "I know it doesn't seem like it because of the way he looks, but according to vital signs and lab values, he really is coming along. Better than we had even dared hope." She shook her head slightly. "The human body is an amazing piece of work. It can take a lot of punishment and then work desperately to heal itself with the help of all this, of course." Her hand made a sweeping motion toward all the equipment surrounding the man. A beeper went off in one of Carlee's pockets, and she stood to excuse herself. Before she left the room, she said, "Mrs. Boresman, I am praying for your husband and for you. I pray for all my patients."

Chapter 13

In a semi-conscious state, Paul could hear conversations, but they seemed distant and not applicable to him. He recognized Jennifer's voice and was reassured; but the nurse, Carlee, an unusual name, seemed vaguely familiar to him. Before he could contemplate it further, he drifted off. The voices quieted, and silence settled on his ears, and he slept.

Jennifer thanked her, and she meant it. *Prayer.* She hadn't thought much about prayer in her adult life. Over the last few days, there had been some desperate cries to God to save her husband, but she didn't imagine that they would be answered. She was too embarrassed to have the chaplain visit when it was offered. She had declined, saying they weren't church-going people. She had gone to Sunday school when she was a child because the neighbors were willing to take her and her sister. It gave her parents some time to themselves on Sunday morning. She remembered some of the Bible stories, but they seemed like fairy tales and God was always killing someone. She remembered that after a few visits she didn't want to go anymore. She had cried long and hard and told her mother she was afraid of the people there. That was the end of that. She and Paul had no interest in church, and frankly, their lives were so good that they had no needs to speak of. There had been a time early on in Paul's practice when she had questioned him about what he did, the abortion part, and whether it ever bothered him. She remembered that her concerns came during the first few months of her pregnancy with Michael, even before she had felt the first barely discernible flutter that made him a reality to her. She never doubted that a baby was growing inside of her body. Paul had not taken her questions well; in fact, the fervor of his defensiveness put her off so totally that she never brought it up again. They lived the good life; she was as happy and content as anyone could be. Paul knew what he was doing. He was a good man, and she trusted his judgment.

Like an uninvited guest with very bad timing, a memory jumped to the forefront of her thoughts, something she hadn't thought about in a long time. She and Paul had been at a huge community affair when the new clinic had opened; physicians and their wives from some of the other clinics came to offer their congratulations. She had inadvertently overheard a conversation between two women. They were lamenting the fact that now the killing of the unborn was happening right under their noses, and they were supposed to celebrate that! The words were not intended for her ears, and so she moved away quickly, but she had felt a stab of guilt. *Killing the unborn.* She pushed the idea out of her mind and had rushed to her husband's side, grabbed his arm, and clung to him. She remembered that he had asked her if she was okay. She had not answered. Why did that piece of the past spring to life on her brain at this moment?

Chapter 14

An alarm on the monitor broke her thoughts, and she jumped to her feet. Something was wrong; she could see that her husband's heart rate was too fast and very erratic. She heard the words "Code 99, room 240" over the loudspeaker, and she knew Paul was in trouble. Carlee flew into the room and asked Jennifer to step outside for a moment. Suddenly the room was full of people, all doing something to her husband. "What is going on?" she asked as a white-coated doctor and technicians pushed past her. A firm hand touched her arm and led her away from the room. "Your husband is having some heart irregularities, and we need to let the doctors and nurses work. I'm Peter Flanders, the hospital chaplain, and I am here to stay with you if you don't mind." He walked her away from the controlled chaos—but chaos, nonetheless—into a small room outside of the ICU. She was very familiar with the room; she had spent many hours trying to rest on the too-short, too-hard sofa. She didn't want to sit now. The short, thin, and slightly balding man did not ask her to sit but came alongside of her and placed his hand on her shoulder. "Mrs. Boresman, can I pray with you for your husband right now? Would you mind if together we ask God to give the doctors wisdom as they deal with this crisis?"

She closed her eyes, allowing hot tears to flow freely down her cheeks, and nodded for him to pray. She was in no position to refuse.

He bowed his head and simply and quietly asked God to protect Paul and his family. He prayed for the doctors and nurses. He then added, "Lord, we pray for your will to be done. Amen."

A sob escaped Jennifer's lips, and she whispered, "What if God's will is not mine?"

Chapter 15

The man wisely did not answer her question immediately. This was obviously not the time for theology. In fact, before he could formulate a response, there was a knock on the door; and a figure appeared: Dr. Clemens, the physician who had rounded on Paul earlier in the morning.

"Jennifer, let me tell you what's going on. I think Paul is going to be okay. The bottom dropped out of his potassium level, sending his heart into fibrillation. Right now his rhythm is stabilized, and we are replacing the potassium. We gave him a fair amount of sedation, so we aren't going to do any breathing trials today. We'll let him rest. I know that must have been very frightening." He moved toward her and gave her a quick hug. "I'll check back later, and the nurses can call me anytime. I'm right here in the hospital." And he was gone.

For Dr. Boresman, the whole scenario was quite different. He was unaware of the events because, as the efficient medical team worked to restore his heart function, he had an agenda of his own. He had slipped back into the light nothingness and was on a mission to find Carlee. The vast expanse was somehow more familiar, even comforting to him, not as empty as it had seemed when he was there last. "Carlee, Carlee," he called, "if you can hear me, please come back. I want to explain something to you." His voice dropped as his words echoed back at him, bouncing off the surrounding light. "I know you are here somewhere. I know that you are real." He was talking to himself now. His mind filled with fear, not the fear he had experienced in his initial visit but fear that his chances for forgiveness were gone. Carlee had said she had forgiven him, but it was not Carlee that he thought of but God. Carlee had spoken about him. She could help him sort through his confusion. *She knows God, and perhaps she can speak on my behalf, be an intercessor.* All hung on to whether he was dead or not, and of that, he simply was not sure; but in this moment, he knew with absolute certainty that it was with God that he had to make peace. If he was dead, then his chances were gone. He knew that too, but had he not been dead the first time? His thoughts were interrupted by a voice, small and yet distinct. "Dr. Boresman, I am here. You are right to remember that I have forgiven you, but you are right again that it is not with me that you must reckon." He could barely make out her slight figure as she seemed to be drifting away from him. She had less substance than he remembered, or was she far away or were his eyes failing him? "I told you before that you would not remember me, and once you are finally out of the gulf, you will not. I really must go. Thank you for helping me." He could hardly make out the last words she had said, and she was gone. He strained against the light to find some remnant of her, but there was nothing.

Suddenly, a jolt stunned him, then another. The light nothingness became a cacophony of sound: voices, none of which he recognized; activity around him; and pain—brutal pain as he was pulled and pushed. He was aware of a terrible burning sensation in his chest as though it was on fire. Confusion overcame him: a sense of helplessness and fear that something dreadful was happening and he could do nothing but let it happen. Alarms rang in his ears, and machines throbbed; his senses were assaulted relentlessly. Then, just as he thought he would go mad, a familiar warmth flooded his body, the din faded, and he was bathed in relief; he had escaped once more. He let the drugs do their job; he wanted to shout a thank-you for the momentary, blessed interlude that took him away from the suffering. He struggled against unconsciousness; he needed to use this time to think. If he didn't have to spend all his energy on pain, he could think. He didn't really care about what had happened, all the confusion, with him, being the center of attention. He had greater problems. His whole life was scrolling before him on a giant computer screen. The arrow moved him forward from the beginning; some entries were highlighted. He had to look at those, but he had no way to work the cursor. He had to focus; it was so hard to focus.

I want to sleep. I can't sleep. I need to know. He fought the clouds that pressed down on his brain to sedate him. He saw Jennifer, and it was for her that he had to do this. The screen froze; the faces, blurred at first, were looking at him, and they slowly began to grow more distinct. They were faces he knew, not well, but they were definitely familiar. Women's faces, sad, tear-stained visages, eyes burning holes into his conscience. These were patients he had "treated." Yes, he recognized them all! Women, young women, girls, just girls! Their looks were not condemning, not even angry, just questioning. He knew the question, but the answer was not one he could bring himself to give. He was tempted to say it wasn't his fault. He had already given the speech to Carlee. He remembered his defense. It sounded hollow when he first gave it; now he felt embarrassed. The drug-induced fog was closing in, and he couldn't resist any longer. It settled on him like a shroud, and he welcomed it. *Too tired. Later, later. I'll do this later.* The screen went blank, and he slept.

Jennifer sat in the chair beside her husband's bed and watched his heart rate, regular and slowing. The rhythmic beep of the monitor soon lulled her into a light sleep. She was utterly exhausted though it was only eleven o'clock in the morning.

Carlee quietly moved about the room, making certain that everything was in order. She looked at the couple and whispered a prayer, "Lord, please make this an opportunity for your good. Use me." She knew that Dr. Paul Boresman was an abortionist; and though she was very strongly opposed to abortion, she had to set aside her feelings as she tended him and his physical needs. She could be neither judge nor jury for this man, but she knew that God worked in mysterious ways and perhaps—the pager in her pocket began to vibrate.

Chapter 16

Hours had passed; at least he thought it was hours. How would he know? It might have been days or a few minutes. He pressed against the heaviness of his eyes, trying to open them. The brightness shocked him, and he quickly retreated. He tried again; and as he adjusted to the light, he saw indistinct shadows of varying shapes on what he assumed was a wall in front of him. The round one he thought to be a clock, but the face was blurred. He tried without success to make out the time—too blurred. A rectangular board was fixed below the clock, and he assumed that the black smudges were writing. He tried to move his head, but pain in his head stopped him short. He winced to himself but decided to move anyway. In his peripheral vision, he saw Jennifer in the chair next to him. He knew it was her; he thought he caught a whiff of her perfume. She started when she saw his head turn toward her. She was immediately standing over him, her hand on his, and said quietly, "Honey, don't move. You're still on a ventilator, and you don't want to dislodge the tube. Sweetheart, are you there? Can you hear me?"

He moved his fingers under her hand and felt the warmth of her skin on his. He wanted to weep with relief. He was not dead, and Jennifer was here with him. He felt a stinging in his eyes and knew that salty tears were bathing the swollen tissues. Jennifer wiped the tears away and continued to reassure him.

Chapter 17

Days melted into weeks, three and a half to be exact, a lifetime it seemed; and though progress was slow, it was sure. He had no more life-threatening events. Paul's physical injuries were healing, but his spirit remained broken and tender. The endotracheal tube connected to the ventilator had been placed into his trachea to free his nose and face. The slow healing of his ribs necessitated the continued support of the ventilator, especially at night. He was not able to talk, but he could nod yes and no. Often people on ventilators are able to write messages, but Paul's right arm was casted, and the fingers on his left hand were too swollen to hold a pen. He had tried pointing at letters or words, but exhaustion overwhelmed him with any effort. He was assured that once the tube was out, he would be able to speak. He knew that. Sometimes the staff forgot that he was a physician and fully aware of all that was happening with him. He took no offense at their forgetfulness. How could he? He was incredibly thankful for every person who treated him with kindness, kindness he believed he did not deserve. Sometimes guilt swept over him, threatening to suffocate him. He often wept and was unable to communicate that it was not his injuries that caused his agony but the grief tearing deep into his raw conscience. As he required less pain medication and sedation, he spent more time awake, more time for thinking. Jennifer was with him for the most of every day; but as he became more stable, she left for several hours at a time to take care of business at home. His children had gone back to college but called daily to send messages of love and support. He became more familiar with the staff—nurses, doctors, therapists, all wonderful and caring—but one visit that he looked forward to every day was from the chaplain, Peter Flanders. He sat with Paul every morning and would read from the scriptures and then pray. There was never an intimation of judgment from the man; and Paul knew that everyone, by now, was aware of who he was and what his profession had been. Conviction swelled in him often, and he longed to share his thoughts, but he had no voice. He wanted to shout out the battle that raged in him: the battle between how easy it had been for him to go to work every day and take life without a second thought and the conviction that what was legally justified was ethically anathema. The nurses would interpret his agitation as pain or stress and would medicate him for comfort. They couldn't possibly know what a relief it was to escape from his thoughts if only for a few minutes. And there was the incredible kindness of the nurses, one in particular, Carlee. She tended to him as though she were caring for her own father. Though his vision was improving slightly, he struggled with details. Jennifer and his children were the only ones he could see clearly in his mind's eye; they were his, part of him. The nurse Carlee, he could tell, was shorter and thin. He thought her hair was brown, and she kept it pulled away from her face. Sometimes she looked like a boy to him, though her voice was definitely feminine, as were her mannerisms. One day, as she came in very close to his face to change dressings, he had a stab of remembrance. *I know her,* he thought. *I have met her somewhere before and feel a need to talk to her.* However, he couldn't talk, and the familiarity he felt for her quickly faded to a comfortable and comforting patient-nurse relationship. He knew that she had been with him since his admission, and days had passed without him being conscious of anything. That explained why he thought he had met her somewhere, and so he stopped trying to put her into a slot in his memory.

After five weeks of immobility, his legs and arm were healed enough for him to get out of bed to a chair with lots of help. Physical therapists worked daily with him in preparation for the big event, and getting up was no small or painless ordeal. Three people had the task of moving his unyielding body out of what had become his place of refuge. The rigid tube in his trachea needed to be stabilized. He knew the consequences of an accidental removal of that necessary lifeline would mean putting it back in since breathing on his own was not an option yet. As uncomfortable as it was, it assisted his breathing;

and like a drug one could hate to love, he needed that tube. Though the swelling had receded from his eyes, his vision was still blurred. A thin veil seemed to persist. This more than any of his other physical injuries worried him. Not being able to see clearly made him feel insecure. Confidence had been Paul Boresman's demeanor for nearly all his life; and now he felt like a baby, a dependent child without the innocence, helpless but with forty-seven years of life experience packed into him. There was the rub of it all. Every day the attending physician would tell him that if he could breathe on his own without ventilator support for twenty-four hours, he could have the tube removed. Paul would nod; but when the sun dropped to the west, Paul would go into panic mode. He was afraid to be without the tube. His heart raced, and he would become visibly agitated. One nurse in particular, Carlee, would sit at his side and try to calm him; several times she had even prayed for him out loud. When tears of joy flooded his eyes, he knew she mistook the tears for fear; and though he tried to tell her thank you, he failed and the end result was always sedation. What would he say? he wondered. Now that the possibility became probability that he would be able to talk, he felt fearful. All the conversations he had had with himself over the weeks seemed too private to share. What if, when he began to feel normal again, he found himself wanting to go back to business as usual? Something plagued him, a conversation he had with someone; but he couldn't remember who, although the words were burned in his mind as if by a branding iron. Who had he spoken with and when? What if he had only imagined that person? What if all the thoughts swirling in his mind were just a dream? But he felt so sure there had been someone else, someone whose name or face evaded him; but nonetheless a deep conviction was troubling him. He vaguely remembered asking the person, whoever it was, for forgiveness—and he meant it. Had all of what he remembered taken place in his mind? So many drugs had been pumped into him, and he knew that hallucinations were not unusual. But what about God? He remembered wanting to talk to someone about God and what could be done to help him be free from the troubling thoughts that clung to his consciousness like glue, thoughts about forgiveness and/or judgment. Chaplain Pete came to see him nearly every day, and Paul knew that he could help him; but without a voice, he couldn't formulate the question: how could God ever forgive him, and how could he, Paul Borseman, forgive himself? How could he look into the faces of his family and not be utterly ashamed? What about his peers, the men and women with whom he had spent the last more than twenty years? He would be laughed at and mocked out of town when he revealed his questions about abortion, and he would have to do just that at some point. What about his career? He was full of questions that he could not ask of anyone yet, but he had asked these and more of God. And yet he wasn't sure that God was hearing him. He wouldn't blame God if he turned his back on him, turned a deaf ear to his questions. Guilt came at him in swells that threatened to knock him over; shame rocked him with such intensity that he felt as if his heart would burst out of his chest. He needed to talk to someone. He needed to unload his thoughts with someone who wouldn't think he was crazy. Jennifer sat at his side, nurses came and went, technicians took blood, physicians visited, and housekeepers cleaned his room; and no one, not one, had any idea of the conflict, the war that raged inside of his mind. And when he could speak, would he talk about a dream he had or an "out of body" experience? Had he sustained injury to his brain? That would be the question flying through circles of friends and acquaintances. It was a question he had asked himself a thousand times. He had been allowed no visitors except for family and for the time being was isolated from what had been a very close circle of friends and colleagues. As he thought about it later, that was probably a good thing.

Chapter 18

Early on a Monday morning, Dr. Tim Johnson, the hospitalist with whom Paul had become most familiar, sat down at his bedside and began, "Paul, all the breathing trials the therapists have been doing are showing us that you are ready to get rid of that tube. I know it's a scary thought, but trust me. You are going to do just fine. We can give you some light sedation and watch you through the day. I want to do this early tomorrow morning when you are well rested, and between now and then, you'll have a little time to get used to the idea." He was speaking very matter-of-factly, not leaving Paul any room for argument. The doctor knew that fear was keeping Paul from moving forward, but he also knew that sooner than later he was going to have to face it head-on. He continued, "Your body is healing very well, particularly your ribs, and you know that was our main concern. You are going to need quite a bit of physical therapy for your arms and legs, but that will be a piece of cake for you, and you can do that from the rehab center. I am a little concerned about your vision, and once we move you to the rehab unit, we'll get Jim Preston, the best ophthalmologist I know, to do some preliminary exams on you. I think you could be ready for discharge in less than two weeks. The remainder of your physical therapy can be done on an outpatient basis. Are you with me, Paul?" Thoughts were swirling in his head like an out-of-control eddy trying to pull him down, but he nodded and even managed a weak smile. He mouthed a thank-you and fought back tears so hard that he was sure he was blanching or blushing. He couldn't tell which.

When Tim left the room, Paul's mind went wild with fear. He knew his heart rate had risen to a point of concern; and within a short minute, Carlee, his nurse, was at his bedside. "Are you in pain?"

she asked gently. He shook his head. "Do you feel anxious?" He nodded, and she responded by moving a dial on one of his machines while letting him know she was giving him a touch of sedation to calm him. Immediately he felt relief and let her know with a nod that the medication was helping. She sat at the edge of the chair next to the bed and put her hand over his, squeezing it just a little to let him know she would stay until he drifted off. This was a routine with which he had become very familiar. He felt an attachment to Carlee that he didn't have with any of the other nurses. He reasoned that that was not unusual for patients who had been hospitalized for extended periods of time. He would have to remember her when he left the ICU and the hospital altogether. He wondered if he would or if all he had endured would slip away like a dream. As his mind began to slow, he felt the pounding in his chest ease; and once again, he was thankful for the comforting hand that covered his. He would not forget her. As she sat next to him, he knew she was praying for him. She had told him that she prayed for all her patients and she was especially praying for him and Jennifer. She had asked him at one point if he minded if she asked prayer for them at her church. He couldn't express his gratitude in words, but he nodded as vigorously as the endotracheal tube would allow.

  The rest of the day and night were uneventful; and when morning came, Paul remembered that he would be allowed to breathe on his own without the ventilator. He knew he had to try to work with the therapists; he knew he couldn't put off the removal of the tube any longer. When Jerry, the respiratory therapist, came in, he was accompanied by Carlee, the nurse with whom he was most comfortable. Jerry explained the process; and with a little help from the sedation, Paul would be breathing on his own. Carlee smiled reassuringly; and behind her, he saw Jennifer coming through the door. Relief soared in him as she slipped in next to the bed and pulled his hand into hers. After her came Chaplain Pete, asking if he could pray before the tube was removed. Of course, no one objected; and Paul nodded, welcoming the offer. His prayer was simple and comforting, asking God to be with Paul and the staff as the tube was removed. "Amen and thank you," came from the small room now full of people. Jennifer began to tell him what was going on at home, how the kids were doing, and anything she could think of to keep his mind off the stress. The respiratory therapist explained the process and asked Paul if he understood. With a slight nod, he indicated he did. Within less than a minute, the tube was out and out of sight. "Lots of big breaths, Paul," Jerry encouraged. "Later on today, the physical therapy folks will be here to get you up in the chair. Try to relax, and if you need anything, Carlee will be right here." Then he added, "Don't try to talk much yet. Your throat is going to be sore for a while." Paul was free of the tube; but in a sense, it had been a friend. All the thoughts running through his head over the last weeks were his alone. What would he say now about the business he had been doing with God when he was unable to speak? How would Jennifer and his children respond to his newfound faith, the transformation in his heart and mind? And what of his career? His eyesight continued to be blurred. The ophthalmologist reassured him that with time some of the blurriness would clear when the swelling around his optic nerve completely resolved. He could not promise, however, that Paul would have 20/20 vision as he did before the accident. So there was the business of all aspects of his surgical career. Everything was different now, not just his physical eyesight but his spiritual eyesight. He could never return to performing abortions even if his eyes were perfect. And without perfect eyesight, he would not be able to perform *any* surgical procedures, even those that were necessary and justified. He did not need anyone to tell him that what he had been doing for so many years was an offense to both God and man.

When he was able to speak, Chaplain Pete was there to hear him pour out all the questions he had, the answers he needed. They spent many hours together, and Paul was finally able to find peace as the chaplain opened the scriptures for him and together they prayed.

Chapter 19

Chaplain Pete had read to him over and over the story of Saul and his conversion. Though he was not comparing himself with the apostle, he loved to hear about how the man had experienced grace and forgiveness and how the fruit of those things in his life lead him to obedience to serve the Lord Jesus as long as he had breath. Saul had done what he believed God wanted him to do, to protect his precious Judaism from the new sect that had arisen after the followers of Jesus began to preach about the Way. Paul, the apostle, however, in his testimonies reminded people of what he had done to the new Christians, how he had persecuted and sentenced to death members of the church unrelentingly until Jesus confronted him and changed his life.

Dr. Paul Borseman would live the rest of his life with the knowledge of what he had done, believing that the law and society had been on his side but ethically he had come to see that there was *no justification* for what he had been doing and calling it health care. The blindness that had veiled his thinking was clearly gone, and he saw with new spiritual eyes that what had been the larger part of his career was one of taking the lives of innocents. And worse yet, he grieved over how he had convinced girls and women that ending their pregnancies would be the right thing to do. He, like Saul, experienced forgiveness and the vastness of God's grace. For that, he would be eternally grateful. How he would serve was yet to be discovered.

Epilogue

After nearly a month in a rehabilitation center, Dr. Boresman was able to walk with the assistance of a cane; and though he still experienced weakness in his right arm, it was not debilitating. His vision was improved enough for him to function; but a slight haziness remained, making it difficult for him to read for extended periods. The ophthalmologist was not optimistic about the haziness going away because of the formation of scar tissue around his optic nerve. Time would tell.

The auto accident had not been his fault; so between reparations from the insurance companies and temporary disability payments he received until he was able to work again, he and Jennifer had no immediate financial concerns. Though Jennifer had never had to work, she was prepared to find some part-time work doing home decorating consultation; but until Paul was completely independent, she opted to stay at home.

When Paul had shared with his family about his conversion experience, Jennifer eagerly gave her life to Christ and rejoiced not just in her husband's physical healing but in his changed views on abortion. She confessed to him the concerns that she had had about abortion but because of her love for him, had never made an issue of them. As for his children, they were wary of his newfound faith and wondered if he had not had some brain injury causing him to become religiously fanatical. Paul and Jennifer were convinced that, as they watched their parents live out their new faith, their children would come to faith. They prayed for that continually.

When the accident was eighteen months behind him and he felt as near to whole as he thought he would be, he began to think about work. His surgeon's license had expired and would have been revoked anyway because of his visual problems but not his medical license. Chaplain Pete kept in touch with him; and one day, while they were visiting, he suggested that Paul and Jennifer think about starting a pregnancy counseling service since there was nothing like that available in their immediate area. He mentioned also that there was a need for counseling among women who had had abortions and were struggling with their conscience. After much prayer and discussion with the pastors of several churches, they decided it was something they would enjoy doing. It could be a ministry. As time went on, word spread that there was an alternative to abortion available close to home; and before long, Paul found himself to be very busy. Churches were calling for him to give his testimony, and he was eager to share. However, the question was always asked as to when during the critical days, the touch-and-go times, did he come to an awareness of God reaching out to him. He always answered truthfully that he didn't know exactly but that at some point he had a sense of God's presence, a calling out to him, and he had answered. He had a remembrance of conversations about his work that he concluded were with himself, his own conscience speaking to him. God, in those times of aloneness, when he couldn't speak, had laid on his heart a heavy burden for pregnant girls and women who needed to know about another choice besides abortion, the chance to give life to a child, whether with them or with another family. He opted not to share about frequent dreams in which he would be asking forgiveness of someone he thought he knew, but then when he got close enough to hear a response, he would awaken, the dream fading before he could give it more thought. As time passed, the weeks spent in the ICU and all that had transpired there became more like a dream than the reality it was. He was growing in his faith in Christ and immensely enjoying the work of counseling and speaking. Paul Boresman had been invited to God's banquet table and had taken his seat; and when he looked around, he saw that there was indeed always room for one more.

As for Carlee, she had told Dr. Boresman that he wouldn't remember any of their encounter, or at least he would not remember her. She had not said that she wouldn't remember him. She had heard his cry to her for forgiveness and knew that someday, or out of time as we know it, she would meet him under different circumstances and tell him face-to-face that she heard and, of course, did forgive him. For that she was grateful, rejoiced with the angels that salvation had come to him by the grace of the loving Father. They would have all of eternity to debate about different and wonderful things, and joy would unite them along with so many others.

> There was a time when God was suppliant, when he kneeled and prayed and asked a beggar for heart room. Thankfully that time is still now. The Lord is knocking on the hearts of men and women, asking for a hearing. There is no door too big or so heavy that he could not knock it down with the breath of his mouth, but at the door to the human heart, he chooses to ask admittance. Open and the gift of life eternal is ours.

About the Author

Marion J. Roybal (Troupe) is the mother of five children, stepmother of two daughters, grandmother to seventeen, and great-grandmother to two beautiful babies, Charlotte and Hunter.

Marion is a retired registered nurse. Most of her career was spent in two specialty areas, birthing centers and critical care units. Some of the elements of the story she has written were conceived through her experience in both of those areas. Before *Roe v. Wade*, she was required to be in attendance at and assist with abortive procedures, all justified by the well-being of the mother. After the legalization of abortion, already a mother, she found herself at odds with physicians who so readily terminated the lives of viable infants. Because of her faith and personal conflict, she transferred to the critical care unit from which she retired.

She is a strong believer in the grace, mercy, and redemptive power of God in the lives of any and all who are willing to meet with him. She has studied and taught God's Word in multiple venues for many years.

In addition to teaching, she enjoys reading, gardening, and spending time with her husband of seventeen years, Adolph; their very large family; and Milo, their beautiful, loving, possibly spoiled Saint Bernard.

CPSIA information can be obtained
at www.ICGtesting.com
Printed in the USA
LVHW042137160419
614446LV00001B/113/P